Preface
By Dale Maccanti

Few know that the original (mis)adventure of the pumpkin-headed boy named Peter was completed way back in 2011. Tennille Owens and I slaved over a hot keyboard and canvas, injecting the breath of life into our creation. Sadly, despite all our hard work, we couldn't find the right home for Peter. Until now!

Welcome to *The Misadventures of Peter Pumpkinhead.*

Peter was born (conceptually) after I stumbled across a friend's illustration of a spooky, cloaked pumpkin-headed man. Inspired, I began writing stories about a cheeky, adventurous pumpkin-boy. Blissfully unaware my inspiration was based on the villainous incarnation of Halloween, Samhain (children of the 80s might remember him from the animated series 'The Real Ghostbusters').

Being new to the world of indie comics, I had a bit of trouble finding a suitable artist, until a close friend introduced me to Tennille Owens. Her fine art style complemented the Burton-esque children's story I was eager to tell. Fast forward three years and I was looking to produce a second book after the success of *Ink Tales*. It was a no-brainer to publish a Peter Pumpkinhead book, but I wanted to emulate the satisfaction of collaborating with multiple talented artists.

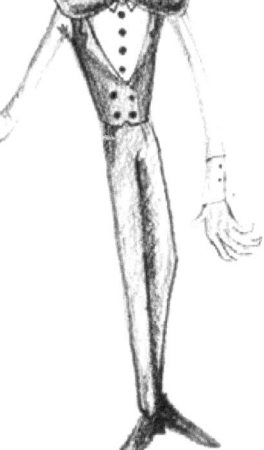

When you flip this book over, you'll be able to read the first 17 instalments of the weekly webcomic, *The Many Misadventures of Peter Pumpkinhead.* In a nutshell, Peter's ongoing journey will be dictated by a new artist every week.

If you can't wait for volume 2 to hit the shelves, head to www.whitecatpress.com

I'd like to take this opportunity to thank all the creators involved, Tennille Owens, Trevor Wood, Nathan Garcia, Glenn Leavold, Caitlin Buckley and the Melbourne Comic Creators Meet Up Crew.

Thanks for supporting the first of many volumes of Peter Pumpkinhead.

Yours proudly,
Dale Maccanti
Editor and Publisher
September 2014

Original sketch of Peter Pumpkinhead by Tennille Owens

The Misadventures of Peter Pumpkinhead

Story by Dale Maccanti

Art by Tennille Owens

Welcome to Spooksville: Population 137. A magical place that exists far beyond our own reality.

Many fantastical tales of adventure and heroism have come out of this small village.

But this story revolves around the misadventures of just one in one hundred and thirty-seven.

Peter Pumpkinhead. Nothing extraordinary about Peter. Just your average pumpkin-headed boy.

Philip Pumpkinhead the Third. Father of Peter. World renowned actor and lover of the arts.

Penelope Pumpkinhead. Mother of Peter. Locally renowned for her cinnamon and worm apple pie.

Life in Spooksville was pleasant for all. Except for one in one hundred and thirty-seven.

As much as Peter wanted to be happy, he just wasn't.

His father was never home because of his busy rehearsal schedule. So Philip tried to teach him the art of acting, but Peter considered it to be too much like lying.

And his mother was too preoccupied with the daily ins and outs of the locals to even notice Peter's existence.

His school life was no better. Being different is a dangerous game when you're twelve. Especially if you choose to wear a black silk bowtie.

Alone, behind locked doors was the only place where Peter felt safe.

But everything was going to change, because Peter had a plan.

A day had gone by and Peter was already in trouble. He had packed some of his mother's infamous cinnamon and worm apple pie, but he figured it was best left until the pain was unbearable.

Finally his luck had turned around and dinner presented itself in the form of a rabbit.

His mother had told him that a rabbit's red eyes were a sign of disease.

But Peter was too hungry to care. A rabbit this plump could last him a couple of days at least.

The potential feast distracted Peter and he didn't realise that he had entered the forbidden forest, where the sacred elm tree stood.

The elders would surely banish Peter forever if they found out about his treachery.

But all Peter could think about was staying alive long enough to curse the black rabbit.

What sorcery was Peter facing? Had clones taken over Spooksville in his absence? Or maybe Peter had travelled back in time without realising it?

All he knew was that his exact double was staring at him, just as frightened as he was.

Then the penny dropped. The sacred elm tree must have led him to a parallel universe. Zombie Jesus had answered his prayers and given Peter a second chance at life.

Peter and newly appointed Peter-Two talked for hours on end until the sun rose. They both realised that the life they desired was on the other side of the sacred elm tree.

An agreement was made that they would trade places. To walk in each other's shoes until it felt like they should return to their normal lives.

Peter was surprised to find that his new parents weren't angry about his disappearance. For in this world, their Peter never left.

Peter noticed a few small changes in this new world.

His father wasn't nearly as famous, which meant he spent a lot more time at home.

And his mother still baked but didn't include anything as vile as worms or maggots, which Peter missed dearly.

His classmates dressed as smart as Peter did, if not smarter. And suddenly, Peter wasn't a misfit anymore. In fact, he was quite popular.

His new life seemed to be perfect. A loving family and friends to play with. It was everything he wanted in his previous life.

But as bright and cheery as the new world appeared, there was something not right with it all

His father was depressed because of his failing acting career. So he resorted to working at the local theatre, hoping one day to be a star.

And his mother strived for creativity with her cooking, but feared being gossiped about behind her back.

Even school had a strange twist of fate. George had become the outcast because his blobbyness stained his shirts.

A month had gone by and despite the fact that Peter's life had improved, the people he cared for were suffering.

Their hugs felt empty and kisses were insincere.

Peter's mind was made up. He had to return home to set everything right. And he knew the white rabbit would lead him there.

Tennille Owens' Panel Process

Thumbnails

Pencils

Colour Test

Final Panel

He didn't dare look back. The temptation to return was too great a risk.

Designing the Cover
By Trevor Wood

I've loved the massive range of styles (and talent, for that matter) that Dale has managed to gather for *The Misadventures of Peter Pumpkinhead*. So when he asked me to do the cover, I was honoured and knew immediately I wanted to incorporate that broad range of styles into my design.

My first draft had a few issues. This being the first collection, Dale wanted it to be more visually engaging. He wanted Peter to appear to be approaching the viewer. My draft was also based solely on the landscape nature of the online strips. We needed to come up with a cover that best represented the original comic and the web series.

Dale was happy with the second concept and wanted to use it for both covers with alternating backgrounds. The next step was to draw it in a few styles. Printing it out, I light-boxed over it with watercolours and pencils, then with inks. Finally I did a couple of versions digitally.

Originally the idea was to have each layer contain a different background but we quickly realised that it made the image too busy. So we stripped it back, using brighter colours to reinforce the amazing range of styles.

I'm thrilled with how it turned out, but more importantly I'm thrilled you picked up this book. Through it you get to see an amazing array of talent, as well as the narrative power of comics. With only 3 panels all these artists have managed to transport you to strange worlds, convey humour, horror and thrills.

And it all came from a single pumpkin seed.

Yours sincerely,

Trevor Wood

1. Initial cover concept   2. Second cover concept   3. Pencil version   4. Paper cut-out version
5. Digital version   6. Watercolour version   7. Ink version

Webcomic Pencils

LUKE ANDREW

NIC LAWSON

YOU BROKE OUR MOON MOBILE!

WHAT'S THAT?!!

OH HEY GUYS

MY STARS!
IS THAT TINA THE GIANT INSANE ASTRONAUT??

I IS SHE INDEED PUMPKIN CHILD. I HAVE BEEN SENT BY YOUR MOTHER TO FIND YOU AND GIVE A MESSAGE...
SHE ALSO GAVE ME PIE...

eek!

IF YOU WANT TO CONTINUE MY ADVENTURE,

HEAD OVER TO WHITECATPRESS.COM

MARIJKA GOODING   SCARLETTE BACCINI   TOM GARDEN

Original illustration of Philip Pumpkinhead by Tennille Owens

THE MISADVENTURES OF PETER PUMPKINHEAD
All stories and art are copyright
© 2014-18 of White Cat Press

ISBN: 978-0-9923465-1-5

Published 2014 by
White Cat Press Pty Ltd
whitecatpress@gmail.com

Publisher & Editor: Dale Maccanti
Art Director: Nathan Garcia
Editorial Assistant: Glenn Leavold
Covers: Trevor Wood

White Cat Press logo designed by Trevor Wood

First printing, October 2014
Printed in Australia

Second printing, March 2018

www.ingramcontent.com/pod-product-compliance
Lightning Source LLC
Chambersburg PA
CBHW042137120726

47911CB00022B/107